BOOGALOO

JEFFREY OTERSEN

To order additional copies of this book, contact:
Xlibris
844-714-8691
www.Xlibris.com
Orders@Xlibris.com

ISBN: Softcover   978-1-6698-1363-7
       EBook   978-1-6698-1362-0

Print information available on the last page

Rev. date: 04/27/2022

This book is dedicated to my family. First, I would like to thank my wife Theresa for helping with the submitting of the story and giving her opinions. Secondly, I would like to thank all my four awesome children: Britney, Brennen, Braiden and Braisley for all the hours of listening and giving their advice and input on this book. Lastly, to Lonnie Dombrowski who wanted to be the monster in this story. At the end of the story, "Boogaloos" name will change to Lonnie, which means "ready for battle."

The story of Boogaloo started out as a Teddy bear story, then I changed it to a Yeti story, then again to an Alaskan Kushtaka Monster story, which I feel is a unique magical story that will entertain a large variety of readers for years to come.

I had a lot of fun and enjoyment in writing this book. Imagining a twelve-year-old boy and a monster, becoming best friends and having an adventure in the Alaskan frontier.

Bing - Bang - Boom! Sounds of marbles crashing off tall pine trees in a hidden forest, on the southeastern banks of Frostburg, Alaska.

A twelve-year-old boy named Sakara takes aim with a slingshot at a target he painted on a tree trunk. Sakara sent a marble soaring through mid-air, striking the target dead center. "Bulls-eye!" shouts Sakara while jumping with joy.

Suddenly Sakara hears the faint voice of his mom calling for him. "Sakara-Sakara. It's time to come home. We have to go to the market." Sakara cups his hands around his mouth and shouts. "I'll be there in a jiffy!" Then he swiftly scoops his marbles off the snow covered ground and puts them in his leather pouch that his Grandfather hand crafted for him with his name bejeweled in colorful gemstones on the front flap.

Sakara jumps on his Qamtik and yells a command, "Mush-Mush!" His team of huskie's rush off pulling his sled fiercely through deep snow towards home. "Whoo-hoo!" he shouts, feeling excited to go to the market where he always gets a special treat for helping his Mom by lifting heavy sacks of grains and flour.

As Sakara zooms across a snowy meadow he hears a loud thumping noise. Then a voice calling his name. "Sakara - Sakara! Come back to the forest." Sakara looks back to the forest but doesn't see any one. He thinks to himself. "That sounded just like my Mom's voice. Sakara gets spooked and races home, skidding into the driveway. He jumps off his sled and quickly climbs aboard the arctic snow machine where his Mom awaits while warming the engine.

Sakara frantically tells his Mom about the voice he heard imitating her voice back in the forest. Sakara's Mom laughs. "That's your mind playing tricks on you. There's no one that lives around here for miles." Sakaras Mom shifts the snow machine into gear and drives towards town on a narrow path through snow that's surrounded by giant snow capped mountains and icy blue waters.

As they near town Sakara sees a sign that reads "FAIR IS ONE MILE AHEAD" Sakara ponders for a moment. "I know how to be fair but I didn't know a Fair was a place too." Feeling a bit confused he decides to ask his Mom. "Mama what's a Fair?" Sakaras Mom chuckles. "I guess you saw the sign back there." Sakara nods. "She explains. "A Fair is a place where people gather to sell and trade goods along with playing games of skill with lots of sweet treats like caramel apples, cotton candy and my favorite elephant ears." Sakara sneers. "Ewww! - Gross. I'm not eating an elephant's ear." Sakaras Mom laughs. "It's not a real elephants ear. It's dough rolled out big and floppy then fried and sprinkled with cinnamon." Sakara smacks his lips. "Mmmm! sounds yummy." Sakara goes on to say. "I guess sometimes words can have a double meaning, depending on how it's used." Sakara's Mom nods "Yes, those are called double meaning words."

Sakara pauses for a moment then he reluctantly asks his Mom. "Can - can we go to the Fair?" Sakaras Mom sighs. "Ahhh! I don't think I have time today, I'm very busy. I have to bake brownies for the school bake sale tomorrow." Sakara looks disappointed "Please - please Mom! This could be my special treat for helping at the market." Suggest Sakara trying to persuade his Mom's decision.

Sakara's Mom sees that Sakara really wants to go to the Fair. She smiles and tells Sakara. "Sometimes you have to stop and smell the roses or life will pass by without enjoying the important things." Sakara laughs "you're not going to find any roses out here in the middle of winter." Sakara's Mom laughs. "Your right, but we will find a Fair." Sakara's face brighten with a smile. "This is going to be the best day of my life!"

After shopping at the market, Sakara and his Mom head to the Fair. When they enter through the gate Sakara is amazed by acrobatic performers dressed in flashy costumes along with clowns juggling flaming fire sticks high in the air. Then Sakara hears loud cheers of people standing in line for a turn to play games for prizes. Sakara spots a giant purple teddy bear dangling from a rope in a large tent along with other stuffed animals. Sakara points to the purple teddy bear. "I really want that purple teddy bear!" Excitedly he shouts as he watches a guy throwing a baseball at steel milk bottles stacked into a pyramid trying to knock them down.

"I know you can do it and win that teddy bear, I have great aim!" exclaims Sakara. "Well let's give it a try." Says Sakara's Mom as they join a long line of people and she gives Sakara a dollar bill then tells him. "It's a going to be awhile before you get a turn so I'm going across the aisle way to look at crafts."

Sakara looks around at all the stuffed animals hanging down with a big tank of goldfish for prizes. The line of people diminishes as people strike out one after the other, going away empty handed.

Now there is one guy standing between Sakara and the game. A big burly man wearing a bear fur coat with the head still attached and caribou boots. He starts his turn throwing the ball mighty fast that knocks down all the steel milk bottles on his first try. "Way to go Kuri!" yells a man from the crowd. Kurri grins ear to ear while pointing to the big purple teddy bear. The carne brings the plush teddy bear down using a long metal rod with a hook on the end then tosses the bear to Kurri. Sakara yells out. "Nooo! That's the bear I want." Nobody can hear Sakara over the loud cheers. Then the crowd of people begin to chant. "Kuri-Kuri" .... As Kuri raises the big purple teddy bear over his head and shouts in a raspy voice. "I always get my bear!" Then he giggles like a hyena.

The carne re-stacks the pyramid and yells "NEXT." Sakara steps up to the counter and hands the carne a dollar for a turn.

The carne gives Sakara three balls and says "Knock 'em all down and you win a prize, Good luck kid!" Sakara picks up his first ball. Feeling very nervous he throws a wild pitch that misses the pyramid. The crowd laughs. Sakara blushes, feeling embarrassed. "This is much harder than it looks." He thinks to himself while concentrating on the pyramid.

Meanwhile off in the distance a Eskimo tribe chases a little brown furry monster running for its life as the Eskimo hunters throw razor sharp harpoons just missing the monster by inches. The monster sees a totem pole with other animal heads carved into the wooden pole and brightly painted, looking realistic.

The little monster climbs to the top of the totem pole and blends in as the Eskimo tribe runs past. When it's clear the little monster climbs down and runs into the Fair. The monster slips into the backside of the knock 'em down game tent and dives into an open box of stuffed animals to hide.

Sakara winds up and throws his second ball as hard as he can but only knocks down a few milk bottles. Sikora picks up his third ball for his last chance to win a prize. He throws the ball fast in a straight line drive, knocking down all but one bottle that rocks back and forth but doesn't fall down.

Sakara looks disappointed. "Ah, that was so close." He thinks to himself.

The carne re-stacks the pyramid and says. "Sorry kid!" Then he yells. "NEXT." Then suddenly Sakara sees a shiny gold coin tumbling end over end in midair, flicked by an older buccaneer that yells. "Give it another try mate! I bloody well know you can do it." Sakara catches the coin one handed. "Thanks Sir!" replies Sakara.

And then he gives the Buccaneer a thumbs-up. Sakara hands the coin to the carne for another try. Sakara picks up the ball and throws a fast curve ball that explodes the pyramid knocking down all the steel bottles Sakara jumps with joy. "I did it - I did it!" he shouts. "We have another winner!" announces the carne. Then he asks Sakara. "What will it be, a kid, a stuffed animal or a goldfish?"

Sakara tells the carne. "I want a purple teddy bear just like the one Kurri won. Purple is my favorite color." The carne looks around at all the stuffed animals hanging down. "Sorry kids, we're all out of purple bears and I don't see anything else that's purple."

Sakara notices an open box of stuffed animals next to an aquarium of goldfish. "Maybe there's a purple teddy in that box." Suggests Sakara while pointing to the open box of stuffed animals. "I'll take a gander," replies the carne as he begins to rummage through the big box. "Hmmm! I don't see any purple teddy's but perhaps you'll like this new quite peculiar stuffed animal." He pulls it up by the tail. "He's not pretty but he's purple!" says the carne with a grin.

The crowd of people let out a loud sigh. "Ohhhh!" They stumble back with a look of terror just starring at the three-foot red eyed purple fury monster with razor sharp claws.

"Look it's a Barney dinosaur," shouts a lady. "That's not Barney, more like his ugly brother the Purple People Eater!" Jokes a man from the crowd. "Whatever it is, it looks real," yells out a trapper. Then an Eskimo hunter yells. "It's Kushtaka, the monster of death!

The carne laughs. "Don't be silly! It's a stuffed animal. They really do a fantastic job at the toy factory making these stuffed animals look life-like," assures the carne.

"It's a baby Kushtaka," yells another hunter. The carne tells the crowd of people. "I'll prove he's not alive," as he takes a metal rod and thumps the monster looking creature in the belly causing a goldfish to pop out of its mouth that is still alive flopping around in midair.

The purple furry monster winks one eye at the crowd with a plucky grin showing his jagged fangs. "He's alive! - He's alive!" yells a frantic lady. "You big buffoon! You just poked a monster in the belly causing him to up-chuck his lunch and now he's going to eat one of us!" yells out a man from the crowd.

The carnes eyes bulge looking dumb founded "Yikes!!" he yelps in a highfalutin voice while dropping the monster to the ground. "Run for your life! He's alive and his breath smells like stinky cheese," yells the carne as he dashes off.

The crowd of people run rampant in a panic, trampling on each other.

Kurri yells. "I want that monster's fur. He's going to make a beautiful coat for my wife!" while trying to aim his bow and arrow at the purple monster.

Another hunter yells. "Not if I get to him first. His head is going to be hanging on my wall and what a story this will be," as the hunter pulls out a machete. Sakara thinks to himself "I must do something before they kill that little monster. Sakara notices the center pole, supporting the tent. Sakara runs towards the pole and does a flying karate kick that knocks the pole out of the ground causing the tent to collapse. Sakara drops to the ground and pulls a mini flashlight from his pouch to search for the monster.

As Sakara gets closer to the monster he calls out. "Hey monster, follow me if you want to live."

The monster is afraid but seems to trust Sakara. He follows him to the photo booth to hide from the hunters. Sakara and the monster go inside the photo booth and see a variety of costumes hanging on a rack next to a long mirror.

Sakara begins disguising the monster with a large Hawaiian shirt and a coat that drapes down over his big webbed feet along with a floppy hat covering his fury otter shaped head and yellow sunflower sunglasses to hide those infra-red eyes. He then wraps a scarf around the monster's pointy snout covering his mouth and neck. Sakara turns the monster towards the mirror. "No one will be the wiser, you now look like an old lady that's completely crazy." They snicker while making funny poses. Sakara then peeps out to see if the coast is clear when all of a sudden the monster presses the start button causing the camera to flash. The bright flash spooks the monster while snapping a photo of the monster with a fierce expression. Sakara calms the monster by hugging him close while telling him with a soft voice "It's okay, no one is going to harm you."

Sakara promises the monster to always protect him. "Cross my heart and hope to die," he swears while motioning with his finger across his heart. The monster nods understanding Sakara, then the monster points to Sakara while motioning a criss-cross over his heart using his fury claw. The two have made a pact to protect each other.

Sakara presses the start button on the photo machine and he begins posing, making funny faces while sticking out his tongue.

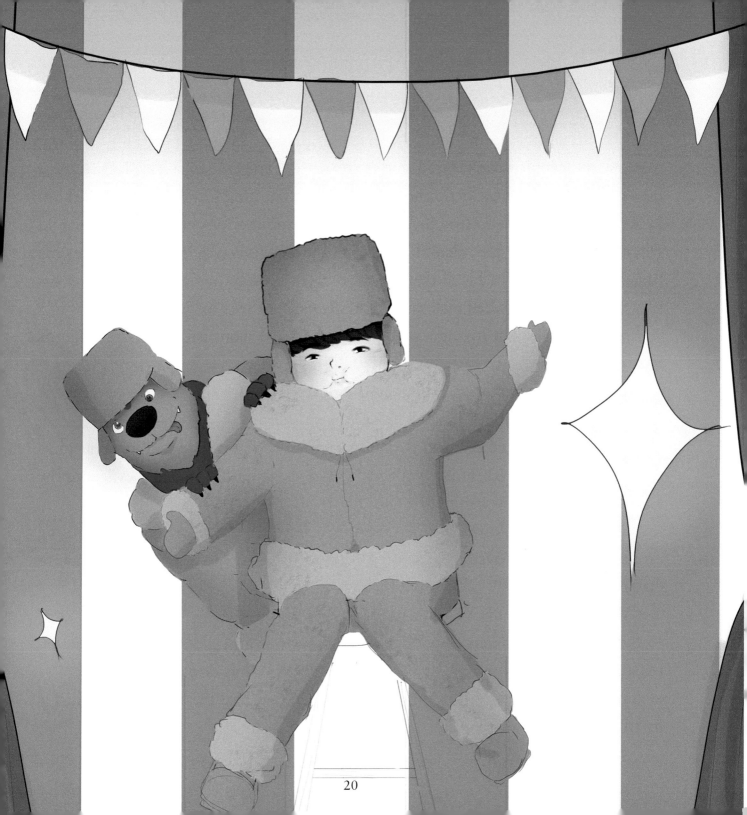

The monster mimics Sakara as the two pose for a variety of pictures. Sakara takes the strips of pics and stuff then into his pocket. Then he peeps his head out to see if the people have cleared out of the area. "The coast is clear, let's make a break for it!" Sakara picks up the little monster, cradling him like a baby. Sakara looks around. "I have to find my mom in this rambunctious crowd of people and when I do you must play dead like a possum, being very quiet" as he places his fingers over his mouth. The little monster nods understanding as Sakara makes his way through the crowded aisle ways. Finally, Sakara sees his Mom.

"Hey Mom look at my new stuffed animal that I won. Isn't it sick!" exclaims Sakara.

Sakara's Mom looks at the disguised monster. "Wow you've won one of those expensive bear stuffed animals. - "Way to go Sakara!"

Suddenly a man's voice abruptly announces. "The Fair is now closed. There has been a sighting of a Kushtaka monster. Please use caution!" People evacuate the Fair running rapid, swarming the exits.

"Wow!" sighs Sakara's Mom. "I can't believe all these people are running around acting kooky over an old foolish folklore - The legend of Kushtaka." Sakara eyes enlarge.

"What is the legend of Kushtaka?"

Sakara's Mom answers "I will tell you just as your grandfather told me but you must not believe in this silly nonsense because Kushtakas don't exist."

Sakara winks at the little monster. "Oh kind of like the unicorn, it's just a myth."

Sakara's Mom agrees. "Yes - exactly!"

Then Sakara's Mom begins to explain the legend of Kushtaka.

"The Eskimo tribes believe Kushtaka is a creature that is half man and half otter that lures people into traps by imitating baby cries. Also they believe the Kushtaka can magically change its appearance, turning into a form of a loved one then disappearing and quickly turning back into a creature that kills. This legend started many years ago by an Eskimo tribe claiming to have seen one.

Ever since then people have been trying to find one but haven't. There's no proof that they exist." Sakara wants to tell his Mom that they really do exist by showing her his new friend but he knows he can't risk the monster's life.

As Sakara's Mom drives towards home Sakara notices little footprints in the snow that follow the snow machines tracks. Sakara then looks at the little monster's foot and realizes it's a match. The little monster followed them to the Fair. When they arrive at home Sakara's Mom asks Sakara. "Did you have fun today?"

Sakara smiles. "It was the best day ever!" As he looks down at his new friend.

Sakara quickly carries the sacks of groceries in the house then nonchalantly carries the little monster to his bedroom then he quickly closes the door and lets out a huge sigh of relief "Wheeeewh! We made it little buddy, we're home, where it's safe," assures Sakara.

The little purple monster smiles feeling safe as he climbs to the top bunk bed to lay down. Sakara begins to question the little monster. "Do you talk?" The monster just grunts. "Do you understand what I'm saying?" asks Sakara. The monster grunts again.

Sakara tells the monster "I guess I don't understand your grunts so I can't expect you to understand English so I'm going to use hand signals and body motions so we can communicate" as Sakara begins using hand language.

Sakara tells the monster, "I have to think of a name for you so you know when I'm calling for you, you'll know it's me," Sakara thinks for a moment. "How about Harry, since you're so furry." The monster makes a sour face. Sakara laughs. "Just kidding! You're right, that's not a good name for you."

Sakara thinks a little longer. "I got it! Since everyone is freighted by you, like the boogieman, so how about the name Boogaloo?" Suggests Sakara. The purple monster smiles while nodding, seeming fond of his new name.

Sakara yawns and climbs up to the top bunk to snuggle up to Boogaloo as the two of them fall fast asleep.

A few hours later Sakara awakes from his nap smelling the sweet aroma of fresh baked brownies. Sakara follows the sweet scent to the kitchen where his Mom is baking brownies. "Mmmm"! Sounds Sakara as he eyes up the big platter of brownies that just came out of the oven. Sakara's Mom tells him. "You may have one brownie, the rest are for the school bake sale." Sakara nods. "Okay Mom, I promise only to eat one." After eating a brownie, Sakara heads back to his bedroom to check on Boogaloo. Sakara notices his bedroom door is open. "I swear I closed it before I left," he mumbles while walking into his room. Sakara looks around his room and doesn't see Boogaloo anywhere. "Oh-no! Boogaloo is gone." Frantically he shouts.

"Who's gone?" questions Sakara's Mom. Sakara pauses for a second. "My stuffed animal that I won at the Fair today. You know the purple hairy monster looking one."

"Oh yes, I just saw that repulsive thing laying on the living room floor," answers Sakara's Mom. Sakara sped off leaping down the stairs to the living room but he doesn't see Boogaloo anywhere.

Sakara heads into the kitchen where he sees Boogaloo sitting at the table scarfing down brownies as fast as he can with chocolate smeared all around his mouth. Sakara snatches the platter from Boogaloo to see nothing but crumbs left. "Wow! You really smashed on those brownies. Now I'm going to be in big trouble!" furiously exclaims Sakara. Just then Sakara's Mom walks into the kitchen while Sakara is holding the platter of brownie crumbs. Sakara looks at his Mom with a surprised look. "Mom it's not what it looks like! I swear I didn't eat the brownies," declares Sakara, sounding innocent. Sakara's Mom gasps. "If you didn't eat the brownies then maybe the cookie monster did!" replies Sakaras Mom sounding snarky.

"I-I-I can explain," stutters Sakara. "Go ahead, I'm listening," replies Sakara's Mom. "It was my new friend Boogaloo. He's really alive. He's a Kushtaka monster. I swear he won't hurt anyone. I saved his life at the Fair when everyone was trying to kill him." Sakara's Mom looks at Boogaloo to see chocolate smeared all over his face. Sakaras Mom bursts out with laughter. "That's clever! That's a good story but I'm not buying it." Sakara tries to get Boogaloo to grunt and move but Boogaloo is lifeless. Boogaloo plays dead like a possum just as Sakara had told him earlier at the Fair.

Sakara's Mom scolds Sakara. "I won't tolerate lying, now go to your room and think about what you did and when you're ready to tell the truth you may come back down." "But I am telling the truth!" exclaims Sakara as he storms off to his bedroom dragging Boogaloo by the arm up the steps.

Sakara goes to his room and slams the door shut while looking angrily at Boogaloo and tells him. "Now I'm in big trouble because of you! My Mom thinks I'm a liar. Why didn't you grunt or move to show her you're alive?" Boogaloo puts his finger over his mouth. Sakara remembers telling Boogaloo to play dead at the Fair.

Boogaloo lowers his head with a sad look, knowing Sakara is mad at him. Sakara feels bad. "I can't be mad at you Boogaloo, you're just doing what I told you to do. I'm sorry Boogaloo! It's not your fault that the carne caused you to up-chuck your lunch - you're probably starving." Boogaloo nods while rubbing his belly. Sakara points to his closet and tells Boogaloo with hand signals that he is going to put food and water in there so when he gets hungry or thirsty he can help himself. Boogaloo smiles. Sakara looks into Boogaloos eyes. "Now promise me you will stay out of the kitchen." Sakara holds out his pinky finger. "Now let's swear on it with a pinky shake." Boogaloo holds out his little finger as the two of them pinky shake. "Hopefully you understand what I said. Now I'm going to teach you how to talk and read - so we can communicate." Says Sakara as he begins to write the alphabet on his chalkboard while sounding out the letters. Boogaloo watches closely and forcefully bellows out sounds.

After a few hours of study, Sakara reads a bedtime story then they fall fast asleep.

The next morning Sakara heads off to school. When he returns he sees his bedroom in shambles. Boogaloo smiles with red lipstick pasted over his teeth while wearing his Moms shower cap. "Oh-no! I'm going to be in so much more trouble!" cries Sakara. He picks up a half-eaten tube of lipstick. "Why did you have to eat it for crying out loud!"

Sakara frantically begins to straighten his room. Boogaloo stands up to help but trips over a box then falls onto his bed, causing him to springboard across the room and lands against the wall while a tall lamp topples over. The lamp shade falls upside down onto Boogaloo's head. Sakara laughs. "Now you have the cone of shame!" Boogaloo laughs along with Sakara.

Then Boogaloo repeats Sakara in a high pitched voice. "I have the cone of shame!"

Sakara's eyes bug out with a shocked look on his face. "You can talk!" Shouts Sakara in utter surprise. Boogaloo smiles. "I can talk!" Sakara tells Boogaloo to repeat everything he says and he does.

A few months later Boogaloo has grown by leaps and bounds standing a little over seven feet tall along with a huge appetite and talking with articulate speech sounding sharp tongue that accents his smart witted humor.

Sakara realizes he can't keep hiding Boogaloo any longer. Feeding him is an all-day chore going out to the forest to gather nuts, berries and wild mushrooms. Sakara tells Boogaloo. "It's time to take you back to the forest where you belong. I can't keep hiding you in my room. You have grown so much, it's just impossible. It's only a matter of time before my parents find out. Plus it's not fair to you to be cramped up in my room all the time."

Boogaloo nods passively looking sad knowing Sakara is right while a few tears stream from his eyes.

The next morning Sakara wakes up early before the sun rises to take Boogaloo back to the wilderness to live.

Sakara and Boogaloo sneak out of the house skirting around bushes and ducking behind trees making their way to the edge of the forest then hiking on a trail that leads up high into the mountains. After hours of hiking Sakara is tired, he sits on a rock to rest while looking out from the mountainous view. "I've never been this high up before. It's awesome! Now we just have to find a cave for you to hide in." Suggests Sakara.

As they both search for a cave, Boogaloo steps into a spring snare trap that hoists him high in the air dangling upside down from a rope looped around his ankle.

Suddenly Sakara hears a voice from an Eskimo tribe that is getting closer.

"Oh - no! They must be following our tracks in the snow. I have to get you down before someone else is wearing your fur. They'll gut you like a fish!" cries out Sakara in a panicky voice. Boogaloos eyes enlarge as he squirms immensely. "I got it!" exclaims Sakara. He pulls out a Chinese star from his leather pouch and throws it accurately, slicing the rope in two as Boogaloo tumbles to the ground. "Well at least it didn't take four tries this time," teases Boogaloo. Sakara chuckles. "I didn't think this time, I just did it!"

Sakara hears the voices of the Eskimo tribes coming from two different directions. "Oh-no! we're trapped, we have nowhere to go. They're going to surround us." Boogaloo swiftly rips a branch off with pine needles from a Sitka spruce tree then scoops up Sakara pulling him in close, tightly into his fur to protect him while using the tree branch to whisk away their footprints. Boogaloo begins to moonwalk.

"Now you see me, now you don't!" utters Boogaloo as they vanish into a snow drift along the mountainside.

It's very cold and dark while the two of them stand still packed in snow as the Eskimos run past the snowdrift.

After a few minutes pass Boogaloo peaks out to make sure the Eskimos are gone Boogaloo steps out of the snow drift lowering Sakara down. "Wow your magic!" exclaims Sakara looking amazed.

Boogaloo shrugs. "Ah, that was an old trick my pop taught me. We used to play a lot of hide'n'seek. Pops always said it might save my life someday." Sakara nods. "It just did! But I was talking about your fur. It changes color like a chameleon." Boogaloo looks at his fur. "Wow my fur changes color so I blend with my surroundings. Oh no I hope I'm not stuck with this color, I'm white as snow. Great! Now I look like the Stay Puft Marshmallow Man!"

Sakara laughs while his eyes are filled with wonder. "So how did you become purple?"

Boogaloo tells Sakara. "That day when I was hiding in the box of stuffed animals I heard you say purple was your favorite color. I just wanted someone to like me."

Sakara gets choked up. "I'd like you in any color, you're my best friend."

Boogaloo smiles "Thanks bro!" Sakara pulls a bag of skittles from his pouch. And tosses skittles at Boogaloo. Boogaloos fur changes color looking polka-dotted in different colors. Sakara laughs. "Now you can blend with a rainbow," Boogaloo laughs. "Thanks for adding some color to my world."

Sakara and Boogaloo hear the voices of the Eskimos. "Oh-no! Their heading back this way informs Sakara. Boogaloo sings out. "Let's beat it!" Then the two of them run as fast as they can through the thick foliage. Boogaloos fur turns back to brown to camouflage with the forest. Sakara points, "Look there's an old cabin probably abandoned from gold prospectors from a long time ago. Let's take a look, maybe we can hide in there," suggests Sakara as the two of them make their way closer.

Sakara walks across the rickety boards that creeks making an eerie sound then he knocks on the door that's covered with spider webs. "Does anyone live here?" Sakara shouts.

The cabin door swings open just a tiny bit as an old man peeks through the opening. "Hello little boy, are you lost?" questions the old man. Sakara answers. "No I'm not lost, my friend and I are looking for a place to hide. The old man opens the door wider looking around. The old man chuckles "Funny thing is I only see you, where's your friend?" asks the old man.

Sakara points over to a big tree. "My friend is hiding behind that tree, we're afraid the Eskimo hunters are going to kill him." The old man looks puzzled as he walks out onto the porch to get a better look. "Please come out from behind the tree, it's Ok I won't hurt you. I promise!" yells out the old man.

Boogaloo steps out from behind the tree. "Aloha" says Boogaloo with a smile.

The old man looks terrified "I'm not sure if you're aware of this but your friend is a snaggle tooth monster! He's going to eat me!" He's looking at me like a one eyed dog in a meat market." The old man runs back inside the cabin, slamming the door with sounds of locks clicking. Boogaloo shrugs "was it something I said? Or is it breathing awareness day? - Sorry, forgot to scope!"

The old man chuckles. Sakara tells the old man. "I promise he's not going to eat you. Boogaloo is a vegetarian. Everyone is afraid of him but the truth is he's more afraid of you because everywhere he goes someone tries to kill him and he doesn't know why. He hasn't hurt anyone or done anything wrong. People are afraid of the unknown."

Then suddenly the Eskimo hunters begin throwing spears at Boogaloo.

Boogaloo starts to dance around dodging the spears Sakara shouts "Please - Help!" The door of the cabin opens. "I guess you're right, young debonair. The world is against him. It's a real phenomenon to see a Kushtaka that talks. He may very well be the last one left. Besides, I'm very fond of him. He's got a great sense of humor. He makes me laugh and I haven't laughed in years."

Sakara and Boogaloo run inside the cabin. "We'll never escape the Eskimo hunters now, they have surrounded the cabin," exclaims Sakara looking troubled. The old man grins. "No worries, I have a grand idea. You two are going to try out my new invention. And by the way my name is Dr. Kluski, like the world famous noodle." "Did you invent the Kluski noodle?" ask Sakara. "No I can't take credit for that, my auntie did." Then Dr. Kluski quickly unveils his invention, pulling the sheet off to reveal an ironing board.

"Ta - da! This is my great invention.`` announces Dr. Kluski, standing proud. "I hate to be a spoiler but the ironing board has already been invented," informs Sakara then he whispers in Boogaloo' s ear. "We're doomed!"

Dr. Kluski replies. "Indeed it has but this isn't your ordinary ironing board. This is a skyboard that will fly across the sky anywhere you want to go." Then Dr. Kluski quickly bolts up a supersonic engine on the back of the ironing board. Next he folds the legs down and tells Sakara. "With this twin supercharger producing nine hundred plus horsepower. You two will soar across the sky like a rocket!" Then he burst out with laughter. "I've finally found a couple of guinea pigs."

The Eskimo hunters bang on the door of the cabin. "Open the door or we'll knock it down!" Demands the chief of the Eskimo tribe.

Dr. Kluski tosses the remote to Sakara then quickly he pulls the rope to crank start the engine.

The powerful whining sound of the super charged engine makes an intense whistle sound.

The Eskimo hunters knock the door down then begin to enter into the cabin.

Sakara and Boogaloo jump on the skyboard. Sakara presses a button as the skyboard lifts up hovering over the Eskimo hunters.

Dr. Kluski yells out. "Hit the boost button." Sakara can't hear Dr. Kluski over the loud roaring engine. "What about my boots?" yells Sakara. "No-No!" The boost button yells out Dr. Kluski. "I can't read the buttons with all the vibration," answers Sakara.

"The red one," yells Dr. Kluski. Sakara quickly pushes the red button, the skyboard engages into high speed while flames spule out of the exhaust pipes as the skyboard jets out the front door then launching high in the air then looping into a huge circle Sakara and Boogaloo's face peel back from the G-force as they race across the sky.

The skyboard begins to sputter as it slows down then stalls out. "Oh-no! I forgot to put more gas into the fuel tank," cries Dr. Kluski. The skyboard plummets to the ground, landing in a big pile of snow. Sakara and Boogaloo pop out of the snow pile. "That was like landing on a giant ball of cotton candy," exclaims Sakara. The Eskimo tribe begin to run after Boogaloo but they are too far away for the Eskimos to catch them.

Sakara and Boogaloo make it back home making sure they weren't followed by the Eskimos.

Sakara tells Boogaloo. "I got an idea, you can live in my treehouse." Boogaloo smiles. "That's a great idea. It would be my own room and when I get hungry I can go out and pick my own berries. Thanks bro!" Then Boogaloo gives Sakara a high-five.

Sakara tells Boogaloo. "You really are a brother to me."

Six months later Boogaloo has grown tremendously, now standing over nine feet tall. Sakara tells Boogaloo. "If you grow any more I'll have to put in an addition to the treehouse." Boogaloo nods. "I'm also going to need an addition to my Hawaiian shirt, it's feeling a bit snug." They both laugh. Then they hear the rumble of a snowmobile pulling into the driveway. Sakara peeks out. "It's my Dad, wow! He has caught a lot of fish. My Dad has been fishing all night. I'm going to help him clean the fish. I'll be back later."

Sakara climbs down from the treehouse. "Great catch Dad!" Sakura's Dad smiles "Come inside and I'll tell you all about my trip." Sakara's Dad hangs the fish on a big hook attached to the fence. They go into the house. A few hours later Sakara comes out to clean the fish but the string of fish are gone. "Oh-no! I can't believe it. Boogaloo ate all the fish!" He says aloud while becoming angry. "That monster can't be trusted," rants Sakara while climbing up in the treehouse.

Sakara slams the door shut on the treehouse and begins to glare at Boogaloo. "What- - what? Is everything okay?" asks Boogaloo.

Sakara shouts at Boogaloo. "Why did you eat all the fish?" Boogaloo looks appalled. "I didn't eat any fish! I swear! Scouts honor" he declares while holding up three fingers - the scouts model.

"Don't try to hornswoggle me. I bet if I belted you in the belly like that carne did, you would spit out fish." Sakara storms off. "I wish you would go back where you belong!" Hollers Sakara as he jumps on his sled and heads out to the frozen lake to replace the fish.

Meanwhile Boogaloo decides to go back to the wilderness to live. "Sakara is right, I just don't belong here. I'm like a fish out of water," mumbles Boogaloo as he packs his belongings into a pillowcase then ties it to a tree branch and carries it over his shoulder. Boogaloo climbs down the tree house ladder. Boogaloo unaware of a picture falling out of his knapsack behind him as he heads off into the forest.

Out on the frozen lake Sakara fishes from an abandoned igloo and he doesn't realize that warmer weather has been melting the ice all day since winter has ended. Sakara catches a string of fish and starts walking across the frozen lake.

The ice creeks and cracks as Sakara tries to walk back to land. All the fishermen have left their igloos. Sakara hears a horrendous loud crack then he falls through the ice. "Help-Help!" he yells trying to get out of the chilly waters.

The Eskimo hunters see Sakara. They try to rescue him by throwing ropes but the ropes aren't long enough to reach him. Meanwhile Sakara's Mom steps out of the house and goes out to the treehouse looking for Sakara and notices the pictures of Boogaloo and Sakara laying on the ground. She picks it and sees the possess. "Ahhh!!" She screams with terror. Sakara's Dad runs out of the house "What's wrong?" he asks frantically. Sakara's Mom shows the picture to him. "That's a Kushtaka monster and it's been living with us."

Then suddenly they hear the cries of help from Sakara. They rush off on the snowmobile heading towards the lake. When they arrive they see lots of people trying to save Sakara but they can't. "Help - Help!!" desperately yells Sakara as he is beginning to drown in the icy waters.

Boogaloo hears Sakara yell for help and comes running from the forest and climbs up a tree and swings out on a long branch overhanging the lake and yells. "Boogaloo is here!" as he plunges into the icy waters to save Sakara.

For a brief moment there's silence then Boogaloo rises up from the chilling waters holding Sakara tightly in his arms. "Look, your fur is blue," says Sakara. Boogaloo gulps. "I guess I'm feeling blue." As he sees the Eskimo hunters point their sharp harpoons at him. Boogaloo lowered Sakara down on the banks.

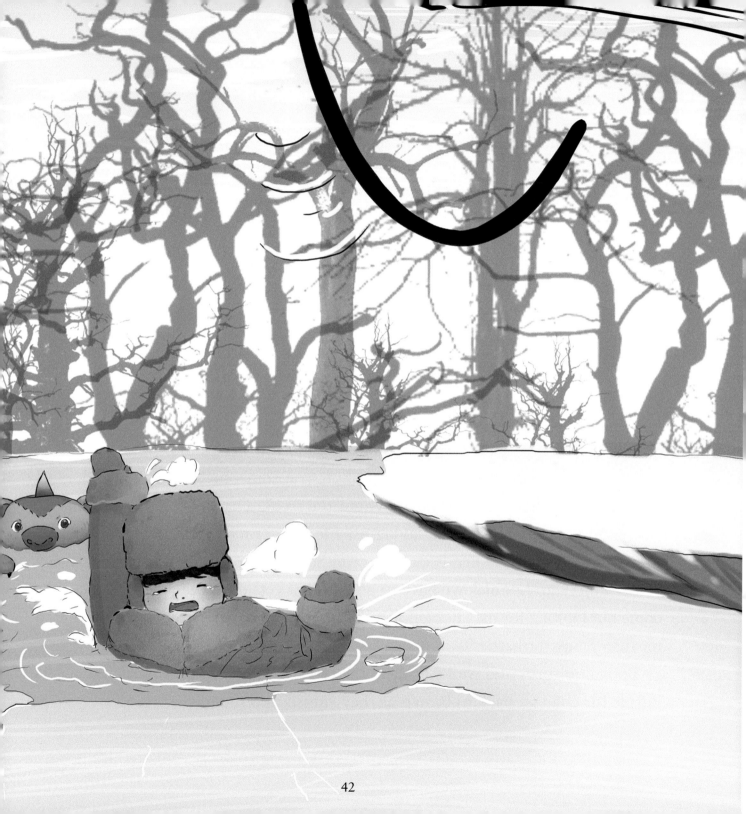

Sakara's Dad steps in front of Boogaloo. "Kushtaka saved my son's life. He is a hero!" All the hunters lower their weapons. "We will no longer hunt Kushtakas. - We were wrong about them." Promises the chief of the Eskimo tribe. Sakara's Mom and Dad thank Boogaloo and hug him.

Suddenly there's a loud thumping noise coming from the forest. Boogaloo tells everyone. "That's my que, I got to go." Boogaloo hugs Sakara. Boogaloo' s fur changes back to purple. "It's time for me to live where I belong, in the forest with other Kushtakas." Tears stream from Sakara's eyes. "I'm sorry Boogaloo. I didn't mean all those things I said. I was just angry at you for eating all the fish my Dad had caught." Sakara's Mom speaks up. "No one has eaten the fish. I took them into the garage to clean them while you and your Dad were talking about the trip." Sakara smiles. "Boogaloo I'm sorry for thinking you were a monster."

Boogaloo shrugs "It's ok. I want to show you someone." He howls and a girl Kushtaka pops her head out from behind the tree". That's Zoey, my soulmate." Boogaloo winks. "Thanks for saving my life many times and taking care of me. I'll never forget you!" Then Boogaloo gives Sakara an exploding fist bump. Zoey yells. "Hurry up Lonnie! We have to go before it gets dark out and all the crazies come out looking for us." Boogaloo tells Sakara. "She prefers the name Lonnie, it means - ready for battle."

Boogaloo turns and walks back to the forest and holds hands with Zoey. His purple fur changes back to brown as they vanish into the forest.

The End

Printed in the United States
by Baker & Taylor Publisher Services